HAD THE COACH GONE LUNAR?

"How in the universe did I make the team, Coach?" I asked. I had just played the worst game of spaceball ever!

"I like your determination, Kar," he said. "I've never seen anyone look as bad as you did out there and just keep playing. But you'll have to work with Grebba Kahn every night after practice. That's if you want to stay on the team."

What a scorch, I muttered to myself.

Like her friends, Grebba was as big as a Pandorian Lootar and probably as much fun as a Blotozoid Zombie. But now that I'd made the spaceball team, I'd do *anything* to stay on it!

Don't miss these other stellar stories of
Zenon, Girl of the 21st Century!

Now available:
Book #1: *Bobo Crazy*

Blasting off to stores in
November 2001:
Book #3: *The Trouble with Fun*

And coming soon:
Book #4: *Stuck on Earth*

ZENON KAR SPACEBALL STAR

BY MARILYN SADLER
ILLUSTRATED BY ROGER BOLLEN

Check out my stellar guide to space station slang on page 84!

A Stepping Stone Book™

Random House 🏠 New York

Text copyright © 2001 by Marilyn Sadler
Illustrations copyright © 2001 by Roger Bollen
All rights reserved under International and Pan-American Copyright Conventions.
Published in the United States by Random House, Inc., New York, and
simultaneously in Canada by Random House of Canada Limited, Toronto.

www.randomhouse.com/kids

Library of Congress Cataloging-in-Publication Data
Sadler, Marilyn.
Zenon Kar, spaceball star /
by Marilyn Sadler ; illustrated by Roger Bollen.
p. cm. "A stepping stone book."
SUMMARY: After sitting on the bench all season, tiny ten-year-old Zenon Kar
finally gets her chance to play spaceball when Grebba, the star of Space Station 9's
best team, is unable to complete the championship game against Earth's finest.
ISBN 0-679-89250-8 (trade) — ISBN 0-679-99250-2 (lib. bdg.)
[1. Ball games—Fiction. 2. Size—Fiction. 3. Contests—Fiction.
4. Friendship—Fiction. 5. Science fiction.] I. Bollen, Roger, ill. II. Title.
PZ7.S1239 Zg 2001 [Fic]—dc21 00-069681

Printed in the United States of America July 2001 10 9 8 7 6 5 4 3 2 1

CONTENTS

1
SPACEBALL CRAZY

My name is Zenon Kar, and I am spaceball crazy.

I was five years old when my dad took me to my first spaceball game. I didn't know anything about spaceball and wasn't sure if I wanted to go. But my dad promised me a Whambama Shake.

"Can I have a Whambama Shake now?" I asked as we walked into the stadium.

Before Dad could say anything, the lights began to dim and a hush fell over the crowd.

In the center of the floor was a huge glass-domed bubble. It was blazing with pink light.

"What is spaceball, Dad?" I asked as we settled into our seats.

"It's a team game," whispered my dad. "It's played by hitting a ball back and forth over a net with the hands."

What's so stellar about that? I thought. But what I saw next was thermo.

The bubble quickly filled up with two teams of players.

Their uniforms shimmered in the light.

Their helmets were gleaming.

They jetted around the bubble and took their positions above the floor.

"They're floating!" I said to my dad in surprise.

"It's a zero-gravity bubble," he explained. "The players move around with jet-packs."

The game began, and one of the players blasted a ball over a glowing laser net.

The ball rocketed back and forth.

Each time it was hit, it lit up in different colors and sparks flew everywhere. Finally, the ball was knocked out of bounds and a point was scored.

The crowd roared with excitement.

Me, I was speechless. To this day, I still get geezle bumps just thinking about it!

After the game, I made an announcement.

"Someday *I'm* going to play spaceball, Dad," I said.

When that day finally arrived, I was ten years old. I was in my fifth year of school at Quantum Elementary.

I thought it was just another Monday, like any other Monday. My best friend, Nebula, and I had just walked through the front doors of our school. We were a few minutes early for class. So we went to the cafeteria to see our friends.

Tad and Var were sitting at our favorite table.

It was the one by the window.

It had the best view of Earth.

"Someday I'd like to go there," said Tad, looking out at Earth. "After ten years on this space station, even *that* place looks good to me."

I knew what Tad meant.

We had lived on the space station all of our lives. Sometimes it felt like the walls were closing in on us.

"The only thermo thing about Earth is the Astros spaceball team," I started to tell them.

But I should have known better.

My friends thought spaceball was inky. Whenever I talked about it, they got all flared-up.

"If you're going to talk about spaceball, I'm going to class," said Var.

"Me too," said Tad.

Sometimes my friends could really shiver me out. It made no sense to me that they didn't like spaceball!

"Cool your boosters," I said. "I'm not going to talk about spaceball."

But it was too late.

Tad and Var were already out the door.

"Maybe we should go, too," said Nebula.

I picked up my data pad and followed her.

Neb and I had been friends forever. But she didn't understand my love for spaceball either.

Then an amazing thing happened.

We were on our way out the door when something on the wall caught my eye.

"Ceedus-Lupeedus!" I shouted.

You're probably thinking that I saw something creepy crawling across the wall. But I didn't. We have our own way of talking on Space Station 9. And "Ceedus-Lupeedus" is what we say when we're surprised.

What surprised me was this sign:

QUANTUM COMETS
★ LOOKING FOR NEW
PLAYERS !!!
★ TRYOUTS <u>TOMORROW</u> AFTER SCHOOL

"You're not serious," said Neb, eyeing me in the inkiest way.

"Well, yeah," I said. "I am."

Nebula looked like she was going to go into global meltdown right there in the school cafeteria.

"Zee, this is lunar. You can't play spaceball! Only girls like Grebba Kahn play spaceball!" she cried.

Then Nebula turned and looked toward the far end of the cafeteria. I turned to look as well.

Grebba Kahn was standing with a few of the other Comet spaceball girls—Tooba Fran and Decca Coom.

They were talking and laughing. *Probably about spaceball*, I thought.

I had to admit they were not the most thermo girls in school. In fact, they were as big as Pandorian Lootars and probably about as much fun as Blotozoid Zombies.

But I wanted to play spaceball, and *nothing* was going to stop me.

2
TRYOUT OF CONTROL

The next day in school, I couldn't stop thinking about the spaceball tryouts.

My teacher, Mr. Peres, had to tell me three times to pay attention.

"I'm sorry, Mr. Peres," I finally said. "I have something very important on my mind."

"Micro-bionics is important, too, Zenon," he scolded.

Micro-bionics is the study of small robots. We use them everywhere on the space station.

Our maid, Woma, is a robot.

Our mailman, Rogo, is a robot.

Even my dog, Bobo, is a robot.

So Mr. Peres did not have to tell me how important micro-bionics was.

"I know, Mr. Peres," I said.

I tried my best to pay attention after that. I even answered one of Mr. Peres's questions about micro-bionic flystroms. But when the last bell rang, I was happy to blast out of there and over to the tryouts.

The gym filled up quickly with spaceball players. The regular team was there, as well as all the players who wanted to try out.

When the coach entered the gym, he wasted no time getting started.

"As you know, we have the best team on the space station," he said, pacing back and forth in front of us.

"But many of our players will be leaving at the end of this year."

I looked around the room.

It was true.

Jon Mon was in his last year at Quantum.

Reeta Swon was moving to Earth.

And Nile Roon was moving to another space station.

"So today we are going to start building our new team for the future!" he shouted. "Good luck to everyone!"

Ceedus-Lupeedus, I thought. *I could sure use a chill chamber.*

We jumped up from the floor and followed the coach into the locker room. One by one, he handed us our practice equipment. When he came to me, he stopped and looked down.

"You are the smallest player I have ever had try out," he said with surprise.

He studied me for a moment. With a

frown, he handed me a jet-pack, a helmet, a jersey, mitts, and shoes.

I put on my new equipment.

Slam! I thought as I looked in the locker room mirror. *Now I know why the coach was frowning.*

My jet-pack drooped down my back.

My helmet dropped over my eyes.

My jersey hung below my knees.

My mitts dangled from my hands.

And my shoes were *two* sizes too big!

"Are you going to be able to play in that outfit?" asked the coach. He sounded worried.

I peered up from under my helmet and said, "As long as I keep my head tilted back, my back straight, my mitts up, and my feet forward in my shoes, I'll be fine, Coach!"

I adjusted my jet-pack and burst into the zero-gravity bubble.

The other players hurried to get out of my way. I was fresh on the court and already out of control.

After that, it only got worse.

With all of my might, I served my first ball.

It cleared the net.

But then so did my mitt.

When the ball was returned, I swung at it with my other mitt. The force of my swing sent me spinning. I crashed into the side of the bubble.

18

"Move up toward the net, Kar!" shouted the coach.

I looked up just as the ball was floating down toward me. It was the perfect setup for a spike. So I hurried up to the net.

Then my helmet slipped down over my face. And the ball bounced off my head.

It must have been funny, because everyone was laughing.

I thought the tryouts would never end. But finally, they were over.

There is no way I made the team, I thought. I felt like I had been swallowed up by a black hole.

Then the most stellar thing happened.

"I have made my decision," announced the coach as everyone gathered around him.

"The following three players have made the team: Simon Gall, Jem Kank, and Pol Sop. In addition, this year, we have one alternate. Her name is Zenon Kar."

1. SIMON GALL
2. JEM KANK
3. POL SOP

3
ALL FLARED-UP

I stood frozen in place.

Had the coach gone lunar?

I had just played the worst game of space-ball ever.

"How in the universe did I make the team, Coach?" I asked.

"I like your determination, Kar," he said. "I've never seen anyone look as bad as you did out there and just keep playing."

"Thanks, Coach . . . I think," I said.

Then the coach fully shivered me out.

He told me I was going to have to work with Grebba Kahn every night after practice.

"That's if you want to stay on the team," he added.

What a scorch, I muttered to myself as I looked over at Grebba.

Like her friends, she was about as big as a Pandorian Lootar and probably as much fun as a Blotozoid Zombie. But now that I'd made the spaceball team, I'd do just about *anything* to stay on it!

That night, I told my parents I made the team. They went quasar! My dad couldn't stop talking about the days when he played spaceball.

He was in the middle of my favorite story—the one about the zero-gravity bubble leak—when my maxi-phone rang.

It was Nebula.

"Zee!" she shouted as she came up on my maxi-screen. "I got tickets for the Microbe concert tomorrow night!"

"Ceedus-Lupeedus!" I cried. "I thought they were sold out!"

"They were," said Neb, "but someone answered my post on the data board."

Microbe was the most thermo group in the solar system. Getting tickets to their concert was stellar beyond belief!

Then I had an inky thought.

"I can't go to the concert, Neb," I said. "I made the spaceball team. Tomorrow night is our first practice."

Nebula was quiet for a moment.

Then she said, "I *guess* I should be happy for you, Zee. But I'm worried you'll turn into a hulk like Grebba Kahn."

Slam, I thought. I couldn't imagine anything worse—then I thought of Tooba Fran and Decca Coom!

"Don't worry, Neb," I said. "That could never happen to me."

The following day, after school, I hurried off to spaceball practice. When I got to the gym, the coach was waiting for me.

"Here's your new uniform, Zenon!" he said, handing me my new jet-pack, helmet, jersey, mitts, and shoes.

I went to the locker room and got dressed.

Then I stood in front of the mirror.

The coach had bought one set of *smaller* equipment, just for me. Everything fit perfectly! *Stellar!*

I raced back to the gym floor.

There's no place else I'd rather be than here, I thought as I jetted into the zero-gravity bubble.

One by one, the coach ran us through our drills. When it was my turn, I flew up to the net. I was ready to make my first move as a member of the team.

Then I heard Tooba Fran say, "Look at her! She's no bigger than a nano-ninny! She couldn't hit a spaceball if it were floating in front of her!"

Tooba got me so flared-up that I missed the ball. The force of my swing sent me spinning in space. Then I spun into the net, setting off the out-of-bounds buzzer.

"She's going to bring down this whole team," said Decca Coom, shaking her head.

The coach looked at me in disappointment.

He turned off the buzzer and sent me out of the bubble. I watched the rest of the drills from the sidelines.

When practice ended, Grebba Kahn was waiting for me. It was time for my first lesson.

She spent the whole time showing me how to use my jet-pack controls.

"If you can learn to use your controls correctly," she said, "you can stop yourself from spinning in space."

"Then what will everyone do for a laugh?" I asked in an inky voice.

I knew I was being scorchy. But I was still

flared-up about Tooba and Decca. And from what I could tell, they were Grebba's friends.

Before Grebba had a chance to say anything, Nebula came running into the gym with Tad and Var.

"Zee, you missed the best concert!" she shouted. "Come to the Mars Malt with us, and we'll tell you all about it!"

Nebula didn't have to say another word.

I was more than happy to blast out of there.

4
GREBBA KAHN

I didn't stay flared-up for long. Spaceball was too important to me.

By the time we met for our next practice, I had cooled my boosters. I ran through the drills without too many problems. Then, afterward, I worked with Grebba.

A few weeks later, it was the night of our first game.

Woma fixed my favorite meal in celebration—spaghetti and beetballs. It looked delicious. I just wasn't hungry.

"I used to get nervous before a game, too," my dad said. "But you'll be fine the minute you blast out into that bubble!"

"Thanks, Dad," I said. "It really helps to hear that."

I was studying one of the beetballs on my plate when my maxi-phone rang.

"Can I answer that, Mom?" I asked. "It could be something about the game."

"Of course, honey," she said.

I pushed my chair away from the table and hurried off to answer my phone.

It was Nebula calling.

"You know I think you're lunar for wanting to play spaceball, Zee," she told me. "But good luck anyway! You'll be stellar out there!"

"Thanks, Neb," I said.

I was lucky to have a best friend like Nebula. She was always there for me.

After we said good-bye, I realized how much I had missed her since spaceball practice had started a few weeks earlier.

My robotic dog, Bobo, had followed me into my room. He floated over and looked up at me.

"I've missed you, too, Bobo," I said, rubbing his fuzzy yellow head. "But now that I've made the team, I've got to see it through."

After dinner, my parents and I left for the game. Dad helped me carry my equipment. He had the most stellar smile on his face.

"I can't think of anything more fun than watching my little girl play spaceball," he teased.

When we got to the game, my parents wished me good luck. Then they climbed up into the stands to sit with my friends.

"Go, Zee!" I heard Nebula shout.

The lights dimmed, and the zero-gravity bubble filled up with pink light.

Players from both teams flew onto the court. All of the players were stellar. But we had Grebba Kahn on our team. She blasted around the court batting balls like a comet on fire!

As the minutes ticked off the clock, I kept my eyes on the coach. Every time he got ready to put in a new player, my hopes soared. But each time, he chose someone else.

When the final bell rang, I was still sitting on the bench. My friends came down from their seats.

"That was as inky as I thought it would be," said Var.

"Why do you want to be on the spaceball team if you don't get to play?" asked Neb.

I was just about to answer her question when my parents rushed up.

"I think I'll have a little talk with the coach," my dad said. He looked all flared-up.

"Honey, I don't think that's such a good idea," my mom told him. Then she plopped my dad's stress reducer on his head and hurried him out of the gym.

I was happy to see them go.

There is nothing inkier than a dad in global meltdown. Besides, I wanted to go to the Mars Malt with my friends.

But when I turned around to find them, they were gone!

What a scorchy evening!

I felt myself being swallowed up by a black hole. Then Grebba Kahn walked up.

I braced myself for the worst. I knew Grebba's friends didn't want me on the team. So why should she?

But when she looked down at me, she had the kindest smile on her face. Then she said, "Don't feel bad, Zenon. You'll have your chance to play. In the meantime, we'll just keep practicing."

It was the most encouraging thing anyone had said to me. And from the best player on the team!

I was so shocked, I didn't say a word, even as she turned and walked away.

5
PANDORIAN LOOTAR

The next day was Saturday. I thought I would sleep in. But Woma woke me up early.

"There's someone here to see you," she said, shaking me gently.

Who could that be? I wondered, jumping out of bed. I got dressed quickly and hurried downstairs.

To my surprise, Grebba Kahn was standing there in the doorway.

"I know we don't have practice today," Grebba said. "But I thought you might like to hit a few balls."

Grebba had played her heart out the night before. *She's the one who should be sleeping in*, I thought.

"That's a great idea, Grebba," I said. "I'd love to."

Grebba sat with me while I ate my bowl of Snackle Frax. We talked about spaceball the whole time. Then Bobo floated into the room.

"What a cute puppy!" cried Grebba, rubbing his fuzzy yellow head.

"Me like Grebba," said Bobo, turning to look at me.

"I like Grebba, too," I said.

When we got to the gym, Grebba helped me with my equipment.

She checked the controls on my jet-pack and tightened the strap. Then we flew into the bubble.

"Does the coach think I'm too small to play spaceball?" I asked as I served the first ball.

"That's what I asked him after the game last night," said Grebba, batting the ball back.

I caught the ball and jetted closer. "What did he say?"

"The coach is worried that you're going to get pushed and knocked around," she answered.

"Is that what you think?" I asked.

"Well, to tell you the truth, Zenon, I wasn't sure what to think. So I just kept on thinking."

"And?" I asked hopefully.

"And I was thinking about Tad's first-place project in the Space Station Science Contest."

"What? Tad's science project! What does *that* have to do with spaceball?"

"His project was about gravity. The less mass you have, the less gravity has an effect on you."

"So?"

"So gravity can give you an advantage, Zenon. Here, I'll show you. Turn off your jet-pack."

I did.

Then Grebba turned off hers.

"See how you float higher than me? It's because you have less mass than me," said Grebba.

"But I thought this was a zero-gravity bubble," I said. "You know, *zero*—like in *no* gravity."

Grebba laughed. "They just call it that because we can float inside it, like we would in space, where there's no gravity."

I nodded. "So there *is* a little bit of gravity in the bubble?"

"Yes, and if you practice using your jet-pack, then you should be able to float higher, spike the ball sharper, and zoom around the bubble faster than the bigger players. Go ahead, Zenon, give it a try."

I turned on my jet-pack, blasted up to the

net, and spiked the ball with all my might.

Grebba reached out to hit it, but I'd spiked it so well, she missed.

"My point exactly!" She laughed.

Grebba and I practiced all morning.

I began to believe that the things Grebba said were true.

I did have something special to add to the team. And just *knowing* that made me play better.

Finally, we had practiced enough for the day.

"I could go for a chill chamber," I said, floating out of the bubble.

I thought about that for a minute. Then I turned toward Grebba.

"Do you want to come to the Mars Malt with me for a Whambama Shake?" I asked.

Grebba's face lit up like the moons of Jupiter.

"I'd love to, Zenon!" she said. "I just have to stop by Decca's for a minute, and then I'll meet you there."

I was in a stellar mood as I flew through the halls of the space station on my hoverboard. I had just played the best spaceball ever. I couldn't wait to tell my friends.

When I got to the Mars Malt, all of my

friends were there. They were talking and laughing. When they saw me, they all began to cheer.

"Our spaceball star is here!" shouted Var.

I hurried over to their table.

"I just played the best game of spaceball I have ever played in my life!" I blurted out. "You should have seen me!"

My friends got that inky look on their

faces. The look they always got when I talked about spaceball.

Then Tad said, "Zenon, you're turning into a regular Pandorian Lootar!"

"Just like your good friend Grebba Kahn!" added Nebula, pointing toward the door.

Everyone started laughing.

I turned to look. Grebba was standing there in the doorway.

With tears in her eyes, she turned and ran out of the Mars Malt.

6
SPACE STATION CHAMPIONS

"What a scorch that Grebba Kahn is!" said Var. "I hope she doesn't start hanging out here at the Mars Malt."

"I know," said Tad. "She could bring this whole place down."

I wanted to say something to my friends, but I was afraid they would think *I* was scorchy, too.

So I didn't say anything.

I drank one Whambama Shake, then got up to leave.

"See ya tomorrow," I said.

"You're scrubbing this mission already?" asked Tad.

"Yeah," I said.

I walked home from the Mars Malt, carrying my hoverboard under my arm.

I didn't want to get home too early. My mom might ask a lot of questions. And I didn't want her to know that I had been a bad friend to Grebba.

When I got home, Woma put dinner on the table. It was beetball sandwiches. For once, I was glad Dad was all flared-up about something. Mom didn't notice I was especially quiet.

That night, I went to bed early. Bobo snuggled up next to me. He looked very worried.

"No be sad," he told me.

"I won't, Bobo," I said. "I just wish I could be a good friend to Grebba like you are to me."

Bobo and I lay there for a long time.

I gazed out my window at the stars. Then I drifted off to sleep.

The next day, I couldn't wait to talk to Grebba. I wanted to tell her that I was sorry my friends had been so inky.

I caught up with her at spaceball practice.

"I'm sorry about my friends, Grebba," I said. "Sometimes they fully shiver me out."

"It's all right, Zenon," she answered. "I'm used to kids making fun of me because of my size."

Then she smiled and added, "I guess it's like *my* friends making fun of *you* because of *your* size!"

We slammed our hands together in agreement. The force of our contact sent us both spinning into the air laughing.

It must have been a funny sight, because the coach started laughing, too.

After that, Grebba and I were closer than ever. We practiced every day, and every day I got better.

Meanwhile, the Quantum Comets played on, winning game after game.

Unfortunately, I continued to watch the rest of the season's games from the bench. Grebba even tried to talk to the coach, but he still wouldn't put me in.

You're probably thinking that I had a global meltdown, right? But I wasn't upset.

I loved my team. I cheered for them every game.

I wish I could have said the same for my friends. They still thought spaceball was inky and never stopped complaining about it.

"The games are too long," fussed Nebula. "You should ask about shortening them."

As far as I was concerned, the games weren't long enough.

Our last game of the season was against the Zarkon Rockets. Next to the Quantum Comets, they were the best team on the space station.

Whoever won this game would win the Space Station Division and travel to Earth for the finals.

We got behind early in the game.

Our serves were off.

Our rushes to the net were slow.

Our spikes were flat.

It took everything we had to keep up.

Then, in the last quarter, we exploded.

We racked up point after point in a flurry.

When Grebba scored the final point to win the game, I leaped up from the bench cheering.

We were the best team on the space station!

My parents rushed down and hugged me. They were as happy as I was. Even my dad didn't seem to mind that I had spent the whole season on the bench.

After all, we were going to Earth to play the Astros!

I looked up in the stands for my friends. I was in the mood for a Mars Malt celebration.

But this time, not even Nebula was there.

7
EARTH BOUND

The next day in school, everyone was talking about the previous night's game.

Even Mr. Peres had something to say.

"That was a stellar game, Grebba!" he told her. "Good luck on Earth! Let's beat those Astros!"

Everyone clapped and cheered.

Mr. Peres didn't know that I was on the team. Since I had been on the bench all season, he had never seen me play. So when Grebba told him that I was a Comet, he looked very surprised.

"You must be the smallest player on the team," he said.

"I am," I said with a sigh.

Then Grebba came to my rescue.

"Zenon is one of our best players," she said. "You'll be seeing a lot of her in the bubble next year."

Throughout the day, the excitement at Quantum Elementary grew.

When the spaceball players walked into the cafeteria at lunchtime, everyone started hooting and hollering.

"I don't get it," said Tad. "No one said anything when I won first place in the Space Station Science Contest."

"That's because everyone loves sports, and no one cares about science," said Var.

"That's not true," I said, sliding into my

seat. "I am *very* interested in the effects of gravity. And I thought Tad's science project was thermo!"

My friends were the only ones who were not excited about the previous night's game. All they could talk about was the new Microbe movie.

"It's opening tomorrow night at the Cosmos," said Nebula. "Do you want to come with us to see it, Zee?"

Before I could answer, Captain Plank, the head of our space station, walked into the cafeteria.

"May I have your attention, please," he cried. "First of all, I'd like to congratulate our spaceball team, the Quantum Comets, on their stellar win last night!"

Once again, everyone started cheering.

"And secondly," he said, "in order to support our space station team, every student will be required to attend tomorrow night's game on Earth. The school shuttle will be departing promptly at thirteen hundred hours. Thank you, and good luck, Comets!"

My friends let out a loud groan.

"What about the Microbe *movieeeee?*" cried Neb.

Everyone stopped cheering and looked over at our table.

Tooba and Decca were glaring.

Even Grebba looked upset.

I slumped down in my seat and waited for the bell to ring.

Mr. Peres let us leave early that afternoon. He could tell that our minds were not on our schoolwork.

As I walked down the hall after class, there were signs everywhere.

GO, COMETS!
BEAT THE ASTROS!

I was so excited, I thought I would go quasar.

That night, after dinner, I packed my equipment. I admired each piece as I carefully placed it in my suitcase.

Win or lose tomorrow, play or not play, I was proud to be a Quantum Comet.

8
A MAJOR
ZERO-GRAVITY SPIN

My parents and I left for the shuttle station just past noon the next day. We got a special pass for Bobo so that he could come along, too.

"Bobo go!" he said with excitement.

"You're my good-luck puppy!" I told him.

When we got to the station, I spotted my friends. They looked like they had been swallowed up by a black hole.

So I decided not to sit with them.

I didn't want to sit with my dad either. He was already wearing his stress reducer.

So I sat with Mom and Bobo. *They will help me stay calm*, I thought.

The shuttle was packed with players, parents, teachers, and students. They sang, cheered, and chanted.

A few times, Captain Plank tried to quiet everyone down. But no one wanted to listen.

Me, I sat peacefully between Mom and Bobo. I looked out at the stars.

When we arrived on Earth, I said good-bye to my parents. Then I joined up with my team, and we walked into the spaceball stadium together.

But what we saw inside took us by surprise. The spaceball stadium was *three times* the size of our stadium at home!

Brilliant colored lights were flashing everywhere. And the roar of the crowd made me dizzy.

For once, I was *glad* that I would be watching the game from the bench.

The Earth team won the toss and served the first ball. It didn't take us long to understand why the Astros were the best team on Earth.

Their serves were powerful. Their returns were direct. And their zero-gravity moves were cosmic.

They were also the *biggest* spaceball players I had ever seen!

By halftime, we were twenty points behind.

Our hopes of beating the Astros were fading fast. We walked to the locker room with our heads down.

To my surprise, our coach was calm. He didn't even have a stress reducer on like my dad. He sat us down and spoke softly.

"You are here for a reason," he began as he paced back and forth slowly in front of us. "You are here because you never once missed a practice. You are here because you worked together as a team. You are here because you didn't quit until you mastered every move in the bubble."

Then he stopped pacing and looked at us.

"You are here," he said, "because you are the best spaceball team in the universe!"

At that, we jumped up from our seats and cheered.

"Let's beat those Astros!" we shouted.

We blasted into the bubble with our heads held high.

We were ready to play like comets on fire. But less than a minute into the second half, we had a terrible setback.

The flystrom in Grebba's jet-pack snapped. It sent her into a major zero-gravity spin.

The crowd gasped in horror.

When Grebba's spin came to a halt, she floated slowly out of the bubble.

"I feel pretty inky," she told the coach. "I don't think I can finish the game."

Everyone sat in silence, waiting to see what our coach would do. He walked over to the bench and looked at us.

Then Grebba rushed up to him.

"Coach!" she cried. "Put Zenon in! I've been practicing with her all season! She has all the right moves!"

The coach studied me for a long moment.

"Zenon Kar, are you ready to play the game of your life?" he asked.

Ceedus-Lupeedus! I thought. *How can this be happening to me now?*

9
ALL THE RIGHT MOVES

I could not believe that I was about to play my first spaceball game. And in the biggest game of the season!

I was having a global meltdown.

But I did not want my coach to know.

"I'm ready, Coach!" I said instead.

I flicked the switch on my jet-pack and flew into the bubble. I hoped no one could tell that I was shaking.

The crowd grew quiet as I floated into my position above the floor.

I knew that I looked really small next to all the other players. Then, to my surprise, Tooba turned and smiled at me.

"Good luck, Kar," she said.

"Thanks," I answered in a shaky voice.

The Astros' first serve over the net was deadly. Before I had a chance to swing, it bounced up and off my *helmet*.

Decca came down on it, slamming it over the net for a point.

My face turned red. *Even my _helmet_ is a better player than me!* I thought.

But I would not let that shake me. I forced myself to calm down and focus on the next serve.

When the ball flew near me, I shot right to it and smacked it to the far outside corner of the court.

This point was mine!

Ceedus-Lupeedus! I thought in shock. *How did I move so fast?*

It's the Earth, I realized a moment later.

There was more gravity on Earth than on Space Station 9. So of course there would be more gravity in the Earth's spaceball bubble! It slowed us all down, but it didn't affect me as much because I was so much lighter than the other players!

Grebba had been *right*!

It was a good thing I was small.

After that, I flew around the court like a shooting star.

The ball fired back and forth.

I waited for just the right moment. Then I rolled into the controlled zero-gravity spin that Grebba had taught me.

When I came out of the spin, I smacked the ball over the net.

The crowd roared.

With less than five minutes left to play, we were only two points behind.

Then it was my turn to serve.

If I do this well, I thought, *we will win this game!*

A hush fell over the crowd as I raised my mitt for my first serve.

I slammed the ball down, placing it perfectly between two big Astros players.

They flew to hit it but were too slow. They missed!

Then they pounded into each other and bounced off the side of the bubble.

My next serve was returned.

But my teammates scrambled and kept the ball going until we scored again.

We were now tied with less than thirty seconds left in the game.

I felt myself begin to freeze.

So I looked down at Grebba, sitting on the bench. Then I looked up at my parents and my good-luck puppy, sitting in the stands.

Finally, I looked over at Nebula, Tad, and Var, my very best friends.

When I served that last ball, I hit it harder than I had ever hit anything.

It cleared the net by a nano-ninny.

Then it came blasting back at me!

As the final buzzer went off, I slammed the ball again. It flew over the net toward the one unguarded spot on the court. Three Astros raced to cover the opening.

But it was too late.

The ball soared past them—out of reach!

The crowd went wild. We had beaten the Astros!

10
GREBBA CAN DANCE!

To this day, I still get geezle bumps thinking about the Astros game.

After I scored that last point, Grebba and Decca picked me up and carried me around the stadium on their shoulders.

"You were stellar out there!" they told me.

"We're so proud of you!" cried my mom.

Even my friends were excited.

"Stellar moves, Zee!" shouted Nebula.

"Thermo!" agreed Tad.

Dad tried to remember a spaceball game from his past that had been as exciting.

But he couldn't think of one.

Then my coach shook my dad's hand.

"Zenon loves this game so much, she inspired the whole team," the coach told my dad. "But I was worried about putting

her in to play with the bigger kids."

"I guess you were wrong," my dad said.

"Yes, I was," admitted the coach. "I've never seen anyone move like she did tonight! She's really learned how to handle herself in that bubble!"

"Thanks, Coach," I said, beaming.

The ride home on the shuttle was a blast. Everyone was talking and laughing. I was so happy, I couldn't sit still. I sat with my friends for a while. Then I sat with my teammates.

When we got back to the space station, no one wanted the celebration to end.

"Let's go to the Mars Malt!" cried Nebula.

"I can't, Neb," I said. "I invited my teammates back to my place. Dad is going to make us Whambama Shakes."

Nebula started to flare up.

Tad and Var looked inky.

But I wasn't going to let them shiver me out. "Why don't you come, too?" I asked them.

My friends were quiet for a moment. Then they shrugged their shoulders and followed me home.

That night, Dad made the very best Whambama Shakes ever. Grebba, Tooba, and Decca each had three. Neb, Tad, Var, and I could barely finish one.

After our shakes, Grebba picked up a spaceball and started doing some tricks. She bounced the ball off her head, her knees, and even her elbows.

Each time she hit the ball, it lit up in a different color.

"Turn the lights out!" cried Nebula, enjoying the show.

I hit the light controls and the lights dimmed down. All we saw was a bouncing ball of light!

Then Tooba and Decca got into the act. Before we knew it, the ball was flashing all over the room!

"That's thermo!" shouted Tad.

It was so stellar to see my friends having fun with my teammates.

But the fun didn't stop there. After I turned the lights back up, Grebba, Tooba, and Decca started talking about the Astros game.

At first, I thought my friends would get inky again. But when I looked at them, they were laughing!

It could have been because Grebba was walking around the room like our coach. She talked just like him, too!

"Do Mr. Peres!" shouted Var.

So Grebba paced back and forth and talked about micro-bionics and flystroms.

But when she started talking like Captain Plank, she really had us howling.

"You have to go to the Astros game whether you like it or not!" she cried in his squeaky voice.

Finally, we couldn't laugh any longer. So Nebula put on her Microbe 3D-CD and we danced.

Grebba was as good at dancing as she was at playing spaceball!

"Show me how to do that!" cried Var as Grebba danced around the room.

Before we knew it, it had gotten late. It was time for my friends to go home.

I was sorry to see them leave. But it had been a thermo day. As we walked toward the door, Nebula pulled me aside.

"I'm sorry I've been mean to Grebba," she whispered. "It's just that I've been jealous. I thought you liked her better than me."

I gave Neb a hug.

"*You* are my best friend, Neb," I said. "Nothing will ever change that."

Neb got the most stellar smile on her face. Then she turned toward my teammates.

"We're all going shopping tomorrow," she said. "Would you like to come with us?"

"Yes!" shouted Grebba, Tooba, and Decca all together.

We made our plans for the next day. Then we said good night. As I closed the door, Bobo floated over to me.

"Zenon happy?" he asked, looking up at me.

"Yes, Bobo, I am happy," I answered, rubbing his fuzzy yellow head. "I am the happiest girl in the universe."

11
ZENON'S GUIDE TO SPACE STATION SLANG

These are some of the terms you'll hear when you visit me on Space Station 9:

beetballs
Beetballs are made of mashed beets and bread crumbs. They are delicious with spaghetti.

Blotozoid Zombie
This is a character from one of the scariest movies I have ever seen, *The Night of the Blotozoid Zombies!*

Ceedus-Lupeedus!
This is our favorite thing to say when we are surprised by something we see or hear.

chill chamber
This is a place, like the Mars Malt, where we go to relax.

cool your boosters
This means you need to calm down and take it easy. I have a hard time with this one.

data pads
These are our portable computers.

flared-up
You're flared-up when you're upset and angry. Sometimes your face can turn as red as a solar flare, too.

flystrom
You will find this small piece of computer equipment inside most of our robots and machines. It's part of what makes them work. If you need to know more, you'll have to ask my dad.

geezle bumps

Although these are like goose bumps, we call them geezle bumps. They look like the treads on the bottoms of the shoes we wear, which were designed by Alfred Geezle.

global meltdown

This happens when you get upset and lose control of yourself.

hoverboard

My friends and I go everywhere on our hoverboards! They look just like skateboards, except they hover above the ground and fly.

inked-out or **inky**

This is when you're spooked or scared or when something really gives you the creeps.

jet-packs

Jet-packs are fastened behind your back like backpacks. They are filled with fuel and are operated by hand controls so that you can fly around a zero-gravity bubble when you are playing spaceball.

laser net

These spaceball nets are made up of many laser beams.

lunar (as in "going lunar")

This is the same as going crazy.

nano-ninny

This is a term we learned in micro-bionics. It refers to the smallest part of a flystrom.

Pandorian Lootar

This is a huge monster in a 3-D video game that we love to play.

quasar
When someone goes quasar, like my dad, it means that he is very excited because something has made him happy.

scorch
Something is a scorch if it's a bad, bad thing.

scrub a mission
This is when you give up what you are doing and move on to something else.

shivered me out
This is when something gives you the creeps.

slam
We say this when we're upset. It comes from getting angry and slamming a door.

stellar
If something is stellar, it is the most wonderful thing you can imagine!

stress reducer
This is a helmet you put on your head when you need help calming down. My dad practically lives in his.

swallowed up by a black hole
You can feel like you've been swallowed up by a black hole when you feel really bad about something.

thermo
This is something that is hot, hip, and stellar!

Whambama Shake
No one loves this milkshake more than I do! It's made from whambama berries and ice cream.

ABOUT THE CREATORS

MARILYN SADLER and ROGER BOLLEN have been creating children's books for over twenty years. Their best-selling titles include the Alistair series of books and the P. J. Funnybunny books, published as Beginner Books by Random House. Their many awards include the International Reading Association Classroom Choice Award and a *Parents' Choice* Award.

Marilyn and Roger originally created Zenon for a hardcover picture book. Then, in January 1999, Disney Channel produced *Zenon, Girl of the 21st Century* as a ninety-minute live-action film. It became the #1 most popular original television movie that year for the channel. This has led Disney to create a second Zenon television movie, *Zenon: The Zequel*, which debuted in January 2001 and was the highest-rated movie in Disney Channel's history.